Howie Razor-Tooth
and the
Shark Gang

Bright Sparks ☆

Howie did not like sharks, even though he was one himself.
Sharks always wanted to get into fights and eat someone.
All Howie wanted to do was play quietly with his friends
and enjoy a vegetarian diet of seaweed casserole.

Howie's best friend was his sucker-fish, Lippy.

Wherever Howie went, Lippy went too.

She cleaned his coat and tried not to let him get too sensitive about everything.

One day, they were sitting together among the rocks. Howie was finishing off a drawing and Lippy was reading a **SCARY** book called "Ghosts of the Deep Ocean."

"What was that?" asked Lippy nervously.

"I didn't hear anything," replied Howie. "I wish you'd stop reading that silly book."

Suddenly there was a loud **BANG!** Dark, shadows passed across the rocks
and the water around them became icy cold.
"We're surrounded!" cried Lippy. Howie began to **TREMBLE** .

"So!" said a booming voice. "We meet again!"
As he spoke, ten **HUGE** sharks came out of the shadows. They grinned at Howie,
revealing the sharpest, cruellest teeth in the seven seas.

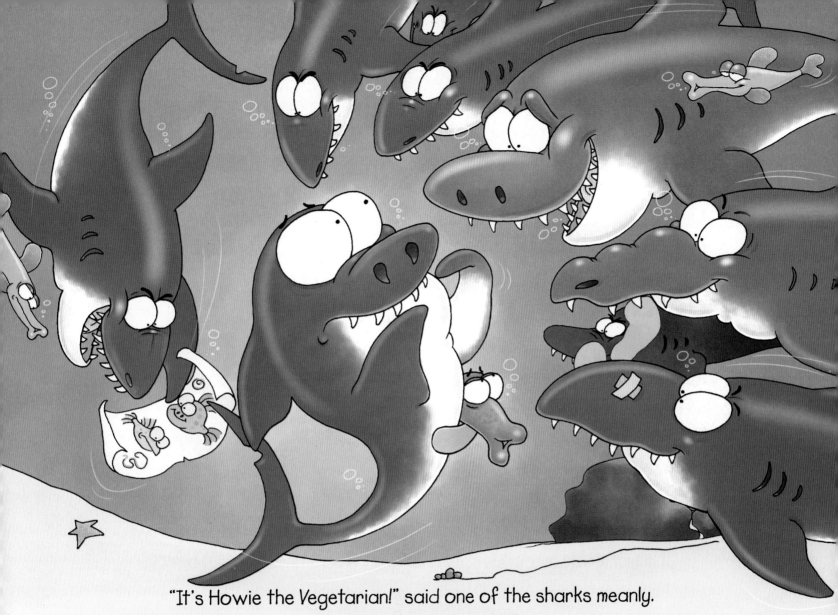

"It's Howie the Vegetarian!" said one of the sharks meanly.

"Howie the Nincompoop!" said another one, and they all sniggered.

"Nice drawing!" said a third shark. The circle was closing in.

"You really must learn how to be a real shark," said the leader in a silky voice. "We only want to help you!"

"I am already a proper shark," said Howie, still **QUIVERING**.

"I am Howie Razor-Tooth and I don't need your help, thank you."

Immediately the sharks drew back with a gasp. "What did you say?" demanded the leader.

"I don't need your help," said Howie, but his voice was wavering.

"No, the first part."

"I am Howie Razor-Tooth," whispered Howie.

"Razor-Tooth!" cried the leader. "Not one of the fearsome,
dreaded Razor-Tooths of the Great North Waters?"

"We are related," squeaked Howie.

The sharks instantly changed their tune.

"He's a Razor-Tooth!" they told each other.

"One of the **_TERRIFYING_** Razor-Tooths of the Great North Waters!"

The leader slapped Howie on the back with a huge, black fin. "You must join our gang!
We would be proud to have a Razor-Tooth amongst us."
Howie didn't want to join the gang, but it seemed wise to be polite.

One by one the sharks came forward to introduce themselves. This took a long time, because sharks like to have long, fierce names to scare their enemies.
"I am Silas the Slayer, Eater of Pirates, Hero of the Siege of Timbuktu and Champion of the Universe!" said the leader.

"I am Bradley Sharp-Teeth, Master of the South China Sea and
Ten-Times Winner of the Sit-Up Cup!"
"I am Armando the Animal, Eater of All Creatures that Live in the Sea
and Breast-Stroke Champion of the South Waters!"
"Nice to meet you all," said Howie. "I am Howie Razor-Tooth."

"Now that we have a Razor-Tooth in our gang we shall be **INVINCIBLE!**" said Silas.

"Time to get into training!"

Lippy had made friends with Silas' sucker-fish, Bob. "Training for what?" she asked.

"No idea," shrugged Bob. "They've been at it for weeks. It gives them something to do."

"Howie draws pictures," said Lippy proudly.

"Really?" said Bob. "I wonder if Silas would enjoy that."

"Let's go!" cried Silas. "Hup two, hup two, get a move on everyone!"
Some of the sharks fell to the ocean floor and began doing sit-ups
and press-ups. One pulled out a pair of dumbbells and started
lifting them **UP** and **DOWN** above his head.

Two sharks pulled great, heavy gloves over their fins and began boxing.
Another one began skipping.

Poor Howie stood there in terror.

"Go on!" said Lippy encouragingly, trying to push him forward.

"What do I do?" said Howie.

"Just copy the others," said Lippy. "You'll be fine!"

Howie tried lifting the weights but they were too heavy. Then he tried jumping over the vault, but he fell over it instead and hurt his nose.

He tried skipping, but the rope got tangled around his fins. He put on a pair of boxing gloves, but he was knocked out in the first round.

"Try some sits-ups!" roared Silas. Poor Howie sank to the floor and tried a sit-up.
Surprisingly, he wasn't bad at it. After a while he rolled over onto his stomach
and did a few press-ups.

"Very good!" cried Silas.

"I've always said that a vegetarian diet was very good for the stomach muscles,"
Howie whispered to Lippy.

After training the sharks huddled together. "Right, here's the plan," said Silas. "We're going to attack the Enchanted City!" Howie was **HORRIFIED**.

He shrank back into the shadows. "We'll creep up on them when they're asleep and EAT up all the mer-folk!""Then we'll eat all their food!" hissed Armando the Animal.

Howie did not wait to hear any more. He turned tail and swam away to find his friends.

"The Shark Gang is going to
attack the Enchanted City tonight!" cried Howie. "We must tell the King!"
"Hmm - the only things sharks are afraid of are killer whales,"
said Oscar Octopus, stroking his chin.

"I've got a plan," said Buster Blowfish, who was always calm and sensible.
"Gather round, everybody."

Meanwhile, the sharks were enjoying a meal of tuna-steaks. They laughed and slapped each other on the back, looking forward to the **ATTACK** that night. Suddenly a great shadow passed overhead. "What was that?" asked Silas, sitting up.

"**_KILLER WHALE!_**" cried Bradley Two-Fins.
The sharks scattered in every direction, not stopping to see that the 'killer whale' was really made up of Howie Razor-Tooth and his friends swimming in formation!
"That showed them!" cried Buster.

When the King of the Enchanted City heard how Howie had saved his people
from the Shark Gang, he held a great feast.
"I knight you Sir Howie Razor-Tooth, Saviour of the Enchanted City and Prince
among Sharks!" cried the King, touching his flaming sword on each of Howie's shoulders.